ANNIE'S choice

Catherine MacPhail

ANNIE'S choice

With illustrations by
Vladimir Stankovic

Barrington Stoke

To my dad, who loved telling us ghost stories

Published in 2014 in Great Britain by
Barrington Stoke Ltd
18 Walker Street, Edinburgh, EH3 7LP

www.barringtonstoke.co.uk

A CIP catalogue record for this book is available from the British Library upon request

ISBN: 978-1-78112-354-6

Printed in China by Leo

Contents

Chapter 1
Omen

It was a dark day when Karam started at his new school.

"I hope it's not an omen," his mother said as she dropped him off. Karam's mother believed in omens. But Karam was more like his dad, who fixed computer problems. Karam and his dad believed in the power of science and logic.

"It's winter," Karam told his mum. "The clouds are filled with rain. That's why they're so heavy and dark."

His mother smiled. He'd never talk her out of her beliefs. "Have a good day, Karam," she said. "I hope you like your new school."

Karam smiled too, but inside he was nervous. He should be used to new schools by now, since his dad's job meant the family had to travel all over the world. And Karam had been lucky so far. He always made friends, but every time he started at a new school there was a small fear inside him that perhaps this time things might be different.

But the playground of his new school was like playgrounds everywhere – children ran and played and chatted. No one even seemed to notice Karam as he stood alone, waiting for school to start. But then a sudden commotion made him jump. A fight had broken out close by. Two boys were locked together, and then one was thrown to the ground at Karam's feet. Karam reached down to help the boy up.

"Leave him be!" the other boy yelled.

When Karam looked up, he saw a boy with angry eyes rushing over.

"I told you to leave him be!" the boy shouted. He stopped inches from Karam's face. Karam stood his ground. He didn't answer, and that seemed to anger the boy even more.

At the same time, a teacher grabbed the boy by the arm and hauled him back. "You're in real trouble this time, Alex," the teacher said.

Even as the teacher dragged Alex away, his eyes never left Karam's. It was only when Alex disappeared inside the school that Karam felt he was able to breathe again.

"I hope you've not got on the wrong side of Alex," a voice said.

Karam turned and found a girl standing beside him. She had a nice smile, and dark hair pulled back in a ponytail. "You don't want Alex as your enemy," she said.

The boy Karam had helped was dusting himself off. "You don't want Alex as your friend either," he said. Then he smiled too. "Thanks for helping me."

Karam looked around the playground. It seemed as if everyone was smiling now. Now that Alex was gone.

"Who is Alex?" he asked them.

"Alex is bad news," the girl said. "I'm Rosa by the way. And this ..." She gave the boy a playful punch in the arm. "This is Paul."

Karam wanted to hear more about Alex, but then the bell rang and there was no more time for talk.

Later, when Alex came back into the classroom, everyone stopped talking. There wasn't a sound. Alex's eyes swept round the class, and rested on Karam. Karam swallowed and looked away. He would avoid this Alex. It was his first day at a new school and he had made two new friends, Rosa and Paul.

But, Karam wondered, had he made an enemy too?

Chapter 2
Darkness

Karam told his parents about Paul and Rosa, but he said nothing about Alex. He knew it would only worry them. Anyway, he would keep well away from Alex from now on.

His father was pleased, but not surprised. "You always make friends, Karam," he said, with a proud smile.

Alex wasn't at school the next day. Karam didn't know why. No one did. But everyone was more relaxed. There were no fights in the playground and everyone chatted happily in class.

"Why is Alex always so angry?" Karam asked Paul.

Paul shook his head. “I don’t know. He wasn’t always like that.”

“I remember him when he was nice,” Rosa said. “Everyone liked him.”

“Then one day ... something just got into him,” Paul said, “and he wasn’t nice any more.”

Karam was puzzled by what Rosa and Paul had told him. “People can’t change so fast, can they?” he asked.

“Alex did,” Rosa said.

“But why?” Karam asked. “Has he got problems in his family?”

Rosa shook her head. “He has a lovely family. They don’t understand either. They’ve done everything they can for him. He’s spoken to the school counsellor and had therapy and everything.”

"Nothing helped," Paul said.

Karam spoke to some other people too, but it seemed no one could see a reason for the change in Alex.

The next day, Alex was back. Karam felt as if a cloak of gloom had been thrown over the school. Alex stood in a corner, his eyes fixed on the ground, looking at no one. He looked so alone that Karam felt sorry for him.

“Keep away from him, Karam,” Rosa warned. “It’s the only way.”

So Karam left Alex on his own in the playground.

But it wasn’t so easy in the classroom.

In the science class, Miss Lewis told them all to get into pairs to work on an experiment. No one wanted to be Alex’s partner. He stood there alone. But Karam didn’t know anyone well enough to be their partner. He, too, stood alone. And so Miss Lewis said, “Alex. Karam. You can work together.”

Karam refused to be afraid. Perhaps all Alex needed was a friend, someone who would trust him.

“Hello, Alex, I’m Karam. I haven’t met you properly yet.” Karam smiled, and his eyes met Alex’s. There was a darkness in those eyes that

Karam had never seen before. A darkness that made him step back.

"You think I care?" Alex said in a whisper. A whisper so hoarse it sounded as if it hurt his throat to speak.

In the same moment, Alex punched Karam and sent him sprawling onto the floor. The teacher ran over to them. "Alex!" she shouted.

Karam looked up at Alex. He was framed against the sunlight at the window. Karam blinked. Just for a moment it seemed that something was standing close beside Alex, shimmering in the light.

Karam blinked again, and the shimmer was gone.

Chapter 3
Chance

Miss Lewis took Karam to the medical room. When Karam looked into the mirror, his eye was black and swollen. Was that really his own face looking back at him?

"Mr Robb would like to see you too, Karam," Miss Lewis told him.

This alarmed Karam. Mr Robb was the headmaster. "Me?" he said. "But I didn't do anything."

Miss Lewis smiled and shook her head. "You're not in trouble, Karam. Don't worry. Not you." As she turned away, he heard her whisper, "Always Alex."

Karam shook a little as he sat outside Mr Robb's office. Only a few days at school and already he had been called to see the headmaster. He tried to think if there was anything he could have done that would have stopped Alex from hitting him. But who or what could ever stop Alex?

Karam shook even more when the door opened and Mr Robb asked him inside. Alex was still sitting in the office. Karam hadn't expected that. He froze in the doorway.

"Come in, Karam," Mr Robb said in a gentle voice.

Karam's gaze never left Alex. He was on the alert, waiting for Alex to leap at him. Alex stared at the floor.

Mr Robb told Karam to sit down. "I have told Alex that you are new to this school, Karam, new to this country – and we should make you feel welcome."

"Everybody's been very nice, Sir," Karam said. His words came out in one rapid breath.

"Everyone except Alex. Isn't that right, Alex?"

Alex kept his eyes on the floor.

"What I want, Alex," Mr Robb said, "is for you and Karam to shake hands. This is a chance for a new start."

Alex said nothing. Karam looked at Mr Robb – his face was pale and tight with anger.

"Alex?" Mr Robb said, so loudly that Karam jumped in his seat. Alex didn't move at all. "Alex!" Mr Robb said again. "Shake hands with Karam. Say you're sorry."

Karam wanted to say, "It's all right. He doesn't need to do this." But he stayed silent. He just wanted out of this room, away from Alex.

"Alex!" Mr Robb's voice had changed. He was almost pleading now.

This time, Alex raised his head – very slowly, until his eyes were staring into Karam's.

'How strange they look,' Karam thought. As if something was swimming in the darkness there, something that didn't belong there.

"Alex, shake hands with Karam," Mr Robb said in a quiet, intense voice.

Karam held out his hand. It shook, no matter how hard he tried to keep it still. Karam saw that Alex's hand was folded into a fist by his side, the nails digging into his palm. He turned away from Karam for a moment, and when he looked back there was a look in his eyes that Karam couldn't understand. One second, Alex looked angry. The next second, he looked scared.

And then Alex yelled, “Keep away from me, Karam!” He stood up and began to back away. “Don’t come near me, and you’ll be safe!”

Then Alex was gone. He ran out of the office with the headmaster close behind him, leaving Karam standing with his hand still reaching out into the air.

Chapter 4
Gallows

"What on earth happened, Karam?" his mother asked when she saw his face. "You weren't in a fight, were you?"

Karam didn't want to lie. He never lied, but he didn't want to tell his mother or father the truth either. And, anyway, he was sure that if he just kept away from Alex from now on, there would be no more punches.

But he couldn't get Alex's words out of his mind. "Don't come near me, and you'll be safe."

What a strange warning. But then, everything about Alex was strange.

As Karam lay in bed that night, he saw Alex's eyes again as they had stared at him in Mr Robb's office. Alex's eyes had looked afraid, almost as if they were afraid of something inside Alex himself.

Karam sat up in bed. It had been as if part of Alex had wanted to shake his hand, but some other part was stopping him. Something so strong that Alex had no power to resist it.

Alex didn't come to school for the next few days. He didn't come back until the day of the class photo.

"I bet Miss Lewis hoped he wouldn't be back for this," Rosa said. "He'll spoil the photo. You wait and see."

Miss Lewis had asked everyone to come to school in their proper uniform, to look smart and clean. Most of them had, but no one looked as smart as Karam. After all, his uniform was brand new, and his mother had made an extra effort. "I want you to set a good example," she had told him.

Miss Lewis was pleased when she saw him. "Oh Karam, you are a credit to the school," she said.

As she moved away, Karam saw Alex walking towards him. "Let him walk past me," Karam prayed.

But Alex stopped beside him.

"Leave Karam be," Rosa said in a cold, hard voice.

Alex shrugged. "Just wanted to say how smart he looks." He tugged at Karam's tie until it came loose. "Oh yes, very smart." He pulled at Karam's shirt. "Oh dear, you've just lost a button." Then he ruffled Karam's hair and laughed. "Oops, not so smart now, eh?" he said.

Karam pushed at him. “Leave me alone,” he cried. “What makes you do these things, Alex? I don’t bother you!”

Alex threw himself at Karam with such force that they both crashed to the ground. “But you do bother me!” he shouted, then he jumped to his feet.

Miss Lewis rushed over. “What’s happened here?” she demanded.

Karam wanted no more visits to Mr Robb. He fixed his tie and patted down his hair. “We just fell, Miss,” he said.

Alex slunk away. Miss Lewis didn’t say anything else. She was keen to get the class photo taken.

The photographer ushered them all into place. Karam saw that Alex stayed right at the back. The teacher said nothing. Perhaps she was hoping he would just disappear.

At last, the photographer was happy. “Everybody smile!” he called. “Say cheese!”

The flash went off, and the photographer checked the image in his camera. “Something wrong here,” Karam heard him mutter. He looked up. “We’ll have to do it again. And you, the boy at the back. How about a smile this time? You look as if you're off to the gallows."

No one had to turn round to see who he was talking to. It was Alex – silent, saying nothing, not smiling, at the back.

Chapter 5
Friends

"If only I could make friends with Alex," Karam said to himself.

Karam found it easy to make friends. He always had. No matter how many times he had moved from school to school, he had never been picked on, or bullied, or even been made to feel left out. Until he met Alex.

Karam wanted to do something about that. His birthday was coming up and his mum and dad had said he could have a party.

So, next day, Karam took his party invitations into school. He handed one to everyone in his class, and then he walked up to Alex and gave him one too. He heard a gasp from Paul.

Alex snatched the invite from Karam's hand and looked at it. "What's your game?" he said.

"Why must it be a 'game'?" Karam asked.

Then Alex's eyes clouded over and he said a strange thing. "If I come to your party, I'll ruin it," he said.

"I'll take that chance," Karam said.

When Alex had moved off, Rosa came over. "What are you doing, Karam?" she hissed.

"I can't invite everybody else in the class, and not Alex," Karam said. "And Alex always looks so unhappy. Perhaps he just needs us to be friends with him."

"He's not unhappy, he's just bad," Rosa said. She sounded a bit cross.

"Have I done the wrong thing?" Karam asked himself, as Rosa shook her head. He would have to wait and see.

Then, just days before his party, there was another shock waiting for Karam when he got home from school. "Karam, your dad is being sent to a new job," his mum told him. "So I'm afraid we'll be moving again."

Karam sighed. He was used to moving house all the time, but he had hoped to stay here for a while longer. It would be nice to make proper friends for once.

"We'll be gone just after your birthday party," Mum said.

Karam told everyone the next day.

"We're all going to miss you, Karam," Miss Lewis said. "You've been a joy to teach."

That same day, Miss Lewis brought in the class photograph. "I'll put one up on the wall to look at," she said. "You need to bring in your money, and then you can have a copy to take home too."

The class all huddled round the photograph.

"Look, I'm blinking!" Rosa said.

"And look at me." Paul laughed. "I look as if I've just eaten something disgusting."

Karam looked at himself. What a sight he looked. Wait till his mother saw him! His hair was ruffled, his shirt was ripped and his tie was all over the place.

It was all Alex's fault.

Karam's eyes searched him out – and there he was, standing at the back, apart from the rest of the class. He had that usual sullen glare on his face.

But there was something else too.

Karam looked closer.

It was as if there was someone else standing close beside Alex. A girl. Was that a face he could see? She seemed to be whispering in his ear. And it almost looked as if Alex was trying to turn away, trying not to hear what that ghostly image was saying.

Karam shook the thought away. How silly! He had too much common sense to be thinking about ghosts. The figure was some kind of double exposure or fault on the camera. It had to be. That was the only explanation.

But as Karam was drifting off to sleep that night, he remembered something strange that had happened the other day in the classroom. Alex had been standing against the light and Karam had seen that same image shimmering around him, as if it was made of spun silver. He was sure it had been the same. It had to be.

Chapter 6
Shimmer

The next day, Karam pointed out the ghostly image to Paul.

"The photographer said there was something wrong, the day the photo was taken," Paul said. "Do you remember? There must have been something the matter with his camera."

"But why only Alex?" Karam asked.

Paul shrugged. "Who knows, but what else could it be?" He smiled. "What do you think it is?"

Karam studied the photo again. He was afraid to say what he thought it was. It sounded silly. But this was Paul, his friend. Paul wouldn't laugh at him.

"I think it looks like a girl. She's bending close, against Alex's ear. Look." He pointed. "Look at her long hair, and can you see a face?"

Paul stared at the photo, then at Karam. "I didn't think you had such a great imagination, Karam. You think Alex is being haunted?"

"That's what it looks like," Karam said. In fact, he hadn't thought of it exactly like that before. "It looks like a ghost."

Now Paul did laugh at him. "You should be a writer, Karam!" he said. "Have you ever thought of writing for *Doctor Who*?"

That made Karam's mind up for him. He wouldn't say anything to anyone else about the image in the photo. Or what he had seen that day in the classroom.

But what was that shimmering image that seemed to follow Alex?

Later that day, Karam saw Alex go up to the class photo and stare at it. He stood there for an age, just looking. Then, all at once, he pulled the photo from the wall and smashed it to the ground.

"Why did you do that?" Miss Lewis shouted.

Alex didn't answer, but Karam wondered ... Had he seen the figure too?

A couple of days before his party, Karam found himself alone with Alex in the changing rooms after PE. "Are you still coming to my birthday?" Karam asked him.

Alex didn't look at him. He shook his head and bit at his lips as if he was trying not to speak. Karam waited for him to say no. Instead, he said, "Yes." Then he looked up at Karam and darkness seemed to fill his eyes. "I wouldn't miss it for anything," he said. It sounded like a threat.

"Had Alex been trying to say no?" Karam asked himself. Was he trying not to speak at all? Because Karam knew that the word – "yes" – that came out wasn't what Alex really wanted to say. It was as if there were two people inside Alex, battling each other to be the strongest.

Karam remembered an old horror story he had read – *The Strange Case of Dr Jekyll and Mr Hyde*. That was what Alex reminded him of. On the outside, there was gentle Dr Jekyll, but on the inside there was evil Mr Hyde, growing more powerful every day until he took over.

Karam shivered, but then he smiled. He was not the kind of boy who made up stories, yet here he was, making up stories.

Alex was still staring at him. "What are you smiling about?" he asked.

"I'm glad you're coming," Karam said.

Alex slammed the door of his locker. "You won't be!" he hissed.

Then he strode off down the corridor, and Karam saw it again.

That shimmer of a shape moving beside him, long hair flowing. Not Karam's imagination. Not a trick of the light.

What could it be?

Chapter 7
Poison

The house was decorated with balloons and streamers and posters. There were banners too. One of them said –

HAPPY BIRTHDAY, KARAM

There was also a long table of party food. Paul headed there as soon as he arrived.

"Leave some for the rest of us," Rosa joked.

Everyone was laughing, everyone was happy. 'All this will change when Alex arrives,' Karam thought, and he half hoped he wouldn't come after all. He was late anyway. So late it would be rude if he appeared now.

But he did.

The door opened and Alex stood in the doorway, a dark shape blocking out the sun.

The music stopped. Everyone turned to look at Alex. Karam hurried towards him.

Rosa stared at Alex crossly. “You’re late,” she said.

“I didn’t want to come,” he said.

“Then why did you?” Rosa asked.

“Because I invited him, Rosa,” Karam said, and he turned back to Alex.

Alex handed Karam a parcel. “I don’t know what it is. My mother bought it,” he said, as if he was sorry even to have brought a present.

“Thank you,” Karam said, but already Alex had pushed past him towards the table of food.

"Just make sure he doesn't poison anything," Paul whispered.

Karam watched Alex for a long time. He never moved from the food table, yet he hardly ate a thing. He only watched, his eyes skimming round the room. And, sometimes, he brushed at his collar, as if he was brushing away an annoying fly.

But there was no fly.

'I must talk to him,' Karam thought. 'If he knows I have seen that strange image, then maybe I can help him. Together, we can make him better.' Karam decided to ask Alex to stay after the party. He would talk to him then.

Karam's mum brought in the birthday cake. The candles were all lit and everyone was singing "Happy Birthday". Karam blew out the candles and everyone cheered and clapped. Then, in that same moment, a hand grabbed his head and shoved it down into the cake.

And Alex said, “Happy Birthday, Karam.”

Karam’s face was covered with sticky icing and cream.

Alex was laughing, but it was a nasty, hollow laugh. “Oh come on, you must think he looks funny,” he said to the rest of the room.

But no one smiled. No one thought it was funny. Alex was the only one who was laughing.

Paul threw an angry punch at Alex, but he dodged it. Then Alex lifted his fist to punch Paul. But Karam was not having fighting at his party. He stepped in front of Alex and grabbed his fist. He had wanted to help Alex, but now he knew it was no use. "I want you to leave," he said.

But when Karam touched Alex it was as if lightning had struck. He felt as if his body was filled with sparks. His heart leapt. The room seemed to spin around him. His head began to swim, and his legs went weak. He stumbled and only just stayed on his feet.

"Are you OK, Karam?" Rosa asked.

"I'm fine ... Just go, Alex," Karam said.

And Alex ran, with his hands over his ears as if he was trying to blot out some great noise he was hearing. But there was no noise. No shouts. No music. Just a huddle of friends gathered around Karam.

Chapter 8
Storm

Paul and Rosa stayed after the rest had gone. They helped Karam and his parents clear up paper cups and plates and the remains of the birthday cake. Most of all, they tried to make Karam feel better.

"I told you not to ask him," Rosa said.

Karam knew she was right, but he still felt dazed, as if there was a mist over his eyes. He almost told them about the electric feeling he'd had when he grabbed Alex's fist, but how stupid would it sound? So he said nothing. Anyway, he wanted them to go. He wanted to be alone.

Karam walked them both to the bus stop, and then he took the long road back home. He needed to think. He was angry with himself, and he was never usually angry. But he had invited Alex to his party and Alex had ruined it. And now Karam had to go into school and face him again. He had wanted to help Alex. He had thought there was a good side to him, a side that was always struggling with the evil that was in him too.

Now Karam dismissed that as nonsense. He had made too many excuses for Alex because he was so keen to see the best in him.

Well, no more.

"I can change things ..."

Karam swung round. "Who said that?" he cried, but he was alone on the street. There was only the chill breath of the February breeze as it rippled through the trees. Karam walked on.

“Let me help you ...” the wind whispered. It had to be the wind, for there was no one else around. Paper and leaves whipped along the street, bare branches like bony arms waved above him, clouds raced across the sky. It was as if the weather was changing. As if a storm was coming. Karam began to run.

Karam was glad now that he would be leaving soon. No more Alex. He wondered if he could pretend to be ill tomorrow so he wouldn't have to go to school, so he wouldn't have to face Alex. "But no," he told himself. "Paul and Rosa will stand beside me. I won't be alone." But that didn't make him any less afraid.

In bed that night, Karam couldn't get to sleep. He tossed and turned and thought about Alex. Karam knew it was because he was afraid to go into school and face him.

"What kind of boy am I to be so afraid?" he asked himself. "Somebody help me!" he pleaded silently. And in the dark of his room Karam heard that voice again.

"Let me help you ..."

Karam sat up in bed, sure someone else was in his room. But there was only darkness. He listened for a moment. Nothing. It had been his imagination. He lay down again and closed his eyes.

"My name is Annie. I can help you ..."

Karam froze. The voice had a name. Annie. He pulled the covers over his head. He was afraid now to look, to sit up, because someone else had to be in the room.

Finally, he had to see. He sat up slowly and looked around. There was no one there. No one. Only the curtains billowing at the window, his desk in the corner, his bookcase by the ...

'Wait a minute – why are the curtains billowing?' Karam wondered. The window was closed to keep out the chill night air. Karam stared and, for a moment, he was sure he saw a figure there behind the curtains – a girl, her face hidden by her long, flowing hair. Her dress almost reached the floor. She looked as if she came from another time. He gasped and blinked. And she was gone.

It was his imagination. Had to be.

Yet, in that moment, Karam was no longer afraid. He lay down and as he finally drifted off to sleep, he heard her voice again. Annie's voice, murmuring close against his ear.

"I know how to help you. Listen to me, Karam ..."

And all through the night, as he slept, Karam listened.

Chapter 9
Annie

The next morning, Karam had no fear, none at all. He must have looked different, too, for his mother asked him, "Are you feeling OK, Karam?"

"Better than OK," he told her. He felt better than he had in weeks, better than he had since he'd first met Alex. He had dreamed all night, dreamed he had heard a voice, whispering to him. She had even told him her name ... what was it?

And, just as he was about to remember, the name was snatched from him.

Karam saw Alex as soon as he walked through the school gates. Alex looked up and saw him too.

"Just ignore him, Karam," Paul told him.

Karam brushed him off. "I know how to handle Alex now," he said, and he marched up to him, bold as brass. Everyone stopped what they were doing. All eyes were on them. It seemed as if everyone was holding their breath.

Alex stared at him darkly. "What do you want?" he hissed.

"I want to tell you it's over, Alex. You can't hurt me any more."

Alex's smile was grim. "Says who?" he asked.

Karam spoke in a whisper. "Says Annie." The name from his dreams came to him at once.

Alex's eyes flashed. "Annie?" he said.

"Yes, Annie. She came to me and told me to tell you to leave me alone. Annie's my friend now."

Karam had expected anger, or at least a puzzled frown. Karam had not expected Alex to smile.

"Annie said that?" Alex said.

Karam tried to think of her exact words. The whisper in the night, the soft hair falling over his face as he slept. Annie.

"Yes, Annie," he said. "She said that I'm Annie's choice now."

Annie's choice? Where had that come from? Where had he heard it?

All of a sudden, Karam was afraid, because he didn't understand what he was saying – or why he was saying it.

"Thank you," Alex said, and that took Karam completely by surprise. "I'm sorry, Karam. I tried to stay back from you. But Annie made me."

Karam shivered. The world was silent. It seemed as if there was no one else in the playground but him and Alex.

"Who is Annie?" Karam asked.

Alex shook his head. "Annie is the dark part of you that wants to do bad things. She'll be in your head all the time now. She'll be whispering, making you do things you don't want to, and you won't be able to go against her. No matter how hard you try."

And, in that moment, Alex changed. He stood up straight. He looked different. "I was Annie's choice and I thought she'd never go," he said. "But now she has you ... and ..." He fell silent and tilted his head as if he was listening for something. "Now I can't hear her." He began to back away. "Can you hear her, Karam?"

And Karam could. He could hear her.

"Don't listen to him," the soft voice said. "He's jealous. I'm your friend now. I'll always be your friend. But you must always do what I say."

Paul came running over. "Wow! Alex is laughing. How did you do that, Karam?" he said.

Karam could hardly hear him. All he could hear were Annie's words, so soft, so close, he felt she was inside his head. "Paul has no right to ask you," Annie said.

"Why do you care?" Karam said.

Paul looked confused. "Karam, you're in a dream."

Karam pulled away from him. "Leave me be!" he shouted, but the voice didn't sound like his own.

"I don't like Paul," Annie whispered.

All at once, Karam didn't like him either. He wanted to hit Paul. He knew he was going to hit him. No matter how hard he tried, he couldn't stop himself.

Paul stared at him. "Karam?"

And Karam punched him so hard that Paul tumbled to the ground.

And now there was a smile in the voice in his head.

“Good, Karam. You’re Annie’s choice now.”

Our books are tested
for children and young people by
children and young people.

Thanks to everyone who consulted on
a manuscript for their time and effort in
helping us to make our books better
for our readers.